Santa's Second Visit

Written by Aysha Reardon
Illustrated by Kerry Shaw

For my precious son Oscar, and the many other
children that celebrate Christmas twice.

The love for you stays strong and true, no matter
what your Mummy and Daddy choose to do.

Last night I rode on Santa's sleigh
and it wasn't Christmas Eve.
Maybe if I didn't have two homes,
then I wouldn't have seen what I see.

So Mummy says that I'm special,
because I celebrate Christmas twice.
Once with Mummy and Theo,
then again with Daddy and his wife.

When Daddy left I was sad,
and worried how Christmas would be.
Would Santa know where to find me?
Would there be presents under my tree?

I thought Christmas would be
lonely with just me, Theo and Mummy.
Would Daddy miss Christmas dinner
and have a hungry tummy?

But then on Christmas evening,
whilst playing with my new toy,
there came a knock at the door,
so I answered and jumped with joy.

"Daddy!" I cried delighted,
as I hugged him oh so tight.
"Come on Champ, let's head home,
for another Christmas day and night".

That's the night it happened,
when I rode on Santa's sleigh.
The night Santa fell from my
Daddy's roof and I had to save the day!
"HO HO HO, hello Jake,
I'm glad that you're awake.
YOU can ride my sleigh tonight,
whilst I take a little break

"Why are you delivering presents again?
I thought you came last night?"

"Oh yes I did," laughed Santa,
"but you're special, isn't that right?!"

"Let me tell you a secret Jake,
there are lots of children like you.
Many special children have two homes,
so I visit them twice too!"

We hopped on the sleigh and
buckled up and Santa called out loud,
"Dasher, Dancer, Prancer,
fly high and do me proud!"

He gave me a wink and passed me the reins,
so I held on super tight.
The reindeer started galloping,
then flew far into the night.

We flew higher than the clouds, high up in the sky, passing many mountains and we even see Dubai!

France was lit up with pretty lights . . .

and Egypt was SO warm!

Iceland was cold and full of snow . . .

After all the presents were delivered, Santa took me home. He gave me a hug and whispered, "You will never be alone."

That was my night with Santa,
riding on his sleigh.
It was such a perfect way to
start my second Christmas day.

So if you're like me and have two homes, you're very special too. Your Mummy and Daddy still love you, no matter what they do.

Santa won't forget you, in fact he'll visit twice.
You may even get a sleigh ride... if you've
been extra nice!!!

Printed in Great Britain
by Amazon